BLUEBERRY BONANZA

by Lauren L. Wohl
illustrated by Mark Tuchman

ISBN: 978-1-943978-29-8

Printed in China

CPSIA Tracking Label Information:
Production Location: Guangdong, China / Production Date: 4/15/2017
Cohort: Batch 68400

Library of Congress Cataloging-in-Publication Data available.

10 9 8 7 6 5 4 3 2 1

Published by

Persnickety Press
120A North Salem Street
Apex, NC 27502

www.Persnickety-Press.com

BLUEBERRY BONANZA

by Lauren L. Wohl
illustrated by Mark Tuchman

For the real Nicholas, the nicest fellow I know.

— L.L.W.

1.

Planting the Story

It's easy to tell this story, because it's not about remembering. Every bit of it is documented—like one of those history programs on television. Melissa Preston took pictures of everything! Right from her brother's blueberry beginning to the day when eight-year-old Nicholas was named the town's Top Businessman of the Year.

Why?

Well, that's the story...

The Prestons are a blueberry-growing family. Mama and Daddy planted ten blueberry bushes in the backyard the first year they were married. They added ten when Melissa was born, and then ten again the year Nico was born. Their patch stretched out over half the backyard. Keeping up with all those bushes was real work, but Nico was a natural, and he loved it.

2.

Maybe It's a Fox

Just last year when he was seven, Nico saved the Preston's blueberry harvest.

In May, when the blossoms were starting to show, Nico, his friend Hannah, and Melissa were on the deck doing homework. Melissa looked up from her books and saw her brother staring across the yard and mumbling.

"Nico, what are you doing?" Melissa asked. "You're supposed to be doing your homework."

"I'm talking," Nicholas answered.

"About what?"

"About blueberries."

"Who are you talking to?" Melissa asked.

He said, "No one," but Nico knew someone was listening—someone big and furry walking in the forest. Nicholas pointed to the woods. "Do you see anything moving?"

Melissa looked. "Nope."

Hannah looked too. She nodded. "I do." Hannah was Nico's best friend.

"Keep looking, Lissa," said Nico.

Yes. Maybe Melissa did see something move. Something dark. Something large.

"Probably just shadows playing tricks on us," she said. After a minute, she added, "Maybe it's a fox?"

"Too big to be a fox," said Nico.

"A deer. It must be a deer."

"Too dark to be a deer," said Hannah.

Finally Nico said, "It's a bear. I've been talking to her."

Hannah added, "Nico talks to her a lot. Sometimes he reads to her."

"How do you know that Hannah?" Melissa asked.

"Sometimes I'm here when the bear comes."

"Maybe that's pretend, Hannah. Nico pretends a lot," Melissa said.

"Not this. The bear is real. I saw her."

"I don't think so, Hannah," said Melissa. "If there were bears hanging around, we would have heard something from the neighbors. Or on the news. Or read about it in the paper."

Nicholas leaned over to Hannah and whispered, "See? I told you she wouldn't believe us."

But Melissa focused her camera and snapped a few pictures anyway. The three of them looked at the pictures. Maybe there *was* something back there in the woods.

"Let's go inside." Melissa pulled Nico and Hannah toward the back door.

"Who will protect the blueberries if we go inside?"

"What are you talking about, Nico? How do you protect them?"

"Last year I made a deal with the bear. I set aside buckets of berries for her."

"But there aren't any berries to give her," Melissa said. "It's too early. All we've got are blossoms."

"Oh, she knows that, Lissa," said Hannah. "But Nico has to tell her that as soon as there are blueberries, she'll get her share."

"And how does he tell her that?"

"He just does."

Melissa didn't know what to say to all of this crazy talk.

"It doesn't really matter now," Nicholas told them. "She's gone. Into the woods."

Hannah and Nicholas went back to their homework. Melissa took some more pictures. None of them showed any signs of bears. She'd print up those first ones, though, to look at them more carefully later.

Weeks later, Nicholas got his chance to talk to the bear. It was just before supper time. He was walking through the rows of bushes, doing his usual check-up—making sure twigs were picked up, branches weren't broken, the screen that they had put up to protect the berries from birds was in place, and the berries were starting to pop.

Suddenly he heard a loud thump coming from the woods, as if a giant acorn had hit the ground. He turned toward the sound. It was no giant acorn. It was a bear. It was The Bear. As big as she was, she had been sitting on a branch in a tree, and something—maybe Nicholas moving around—made her jump down. She was walking slowly, toward the blueberry patch, but she stopped when she saw Nicholas and looked directly at him. He looked right back at her.

"Hello."

She was listening.

"I know you've got your eyes on our blueberries. They aren't ready to eat yet."

She took one step in Nico's direction. It was a big step—a bear-sized step. She wasn't quite in their yard, but as close as she ever came—close enough for Nico to smell her.

He guessed bears didn't take a lot of baths.

She made a low sound. Not a growl, but a kind of soft rumble. It was her stomach. Maybe she was hungry.

"As soon as these blueberries are ripe," Nicholas told her, "I'm going to pick a whole giant-sized bucketful. I'll put it right there. Just the way I did last summer. Those will be for you. The rest are ours, and you have to leave them alone. That's our deal."

The bear turned and walked back into the woods.

"I think that's fair," Nico added.

The bear continued to walk into the woods. She's thinking about it, Nico told himself. She'll see that I'm right.

3.

Bowls and Buckets and Boxes and Bags

It was early August, and the blueberries were big, fat, and about to burst. On a sunny day, the whole backyard smelled like a just-opened jar of jam. It was picking time.

Nico's job was tasting. Not all the berries were ready at once, and he was the one to figure out where they should start their harvesting. He decided on one section of the patch where many of the bushes had berries ready to be picked. That weekend he, Mama, Daddy, and Melissa got started.

They picked all morning, then drank about a gallon of lemonade, ate some leftover chicken, and picked again all afternoon, until they were all too tired to pick one more blueberry. They had five big over-flowing bucketfuls when they stopped. Way more berries than any one family could ever use.

"Wow," was all Mama said as she looked at those buckets and then at all the blueberries still on the bushes.

Mama and Daddy went in to start supper. Melissa pulled the cart with the filled buckets to the sheltered side of the house and covered them with a large canvas blanket.

Nicholas quietly filled their biggest garden pail with handful after handful of blueberries. He struggled to lift the pail. He could only manage to half-carry, half-drag it over to a spot between the last row of bushes and the first row of trees.

"All yours," he shouted into the woods.

Mama came out and called to her children.

"We did a great job today," she said, "but even so, we only covered about a third of the bushes. We've never had this many berries before. I don't know how we'll get all those blueberries picked. Some will probably just rot on the bushes."

"Maybe I can put up a couple of signs and invite our neighbors to help us harvest," Nicholas suggested.

"Great idea, Nico," said Melissa.

"We'll tell them they can keep whatever they pick," Nico added.

"Lissa, we should use some of your photos. We can put the most scrumptious-looking photos on the signs. That will get people over here," said Daddy.

"I'll go upstairs and look through my pictures and

print out the best ones."

"I'll ask Hannah to help me put up the signs tomorrow morning," Nicholas added.

The plan worked. Whether it was Melissa's close-up photographs of blueberries growing or the photos of blueberry syrup dripping down a stack of Sunday-morning pancakes that got them there, lots of people arrived. Whole families came. A bunch of teenagers showed up. Ms. Brody from down the street brought her book club.

Everyone carried bowls and buckets and boxes and bags, ready for filling.

Nicholas was leading the first group to a section of bushes at the back of the patch when he thought he saw the bear watching all the action from a spot in the woods. He stared for a couple of moments—to be certain of what he saw. Yup, she was there, probably wondering what all these people were doing.

Nico had to "think on his feet" as Daddy would say. He turned his group around and announced, "Looks like there are better berries over there." He pointed in the opposite direction. The group followed him, listening as he explained: "There will be more bushes with berries ready to pick over here. Take the darkest, biggest berries. The small, pale ones aren't ready yet."

"Can we eat them while we're working?" one of the book-club members asked.

"Of course," said Mama. "I don't know how you could resist."

"Mama, maybe it would be nice to play some music for everyone while they are working. Something fast. And loud,"

Nico suggested. (He knew the bear didn't like loud sounds.)

"What do you think?" Mama asked everyone.

"Sure. That would be fun. And we'll get the job done faster," one of the neighbors answered.

Melissa took photographs of each group at work, and later of each person leaving with blue-stained fingers, big smiles, and bags and buckets filled with treasure. "What are we going to do with all these berries," one of their neighbors asked. "There are more here than my family can eat."

"I'm going to bring some of mine to the senior center. I'm sure the folks there will appreciate fresh blueberries," another neighbor answered.

"What a good idea," Ms. Brody said. "I can bring some to the park day camp, so the kids can have a healthy snack."

Ooops! That reminded Nico of someone else who was waiting for a "snack." He secretly grabbed a big pail, poured some blueberries into it from several of the filled buckets waiting in the rows, snuck off to the corner of the patch closest to the woods, and set the pail down.

Everyone was so excited, they didn't miss Nico at all.
They were too busy buzzing with great ideas for their overflow
of blueberries.

It got Nicholas thinking. All these blueberries . . .

Melissa was thinking too. She decided to send her
photographs to the Raccoon River Pilot. Sometimes they ran
photo essays about the community working together.

Maybe they'd use hers.

The editor called her as soon as he got the pictures. He said he'd pay her $25.00 to use a few of the photographs if she would also write a story about the day.

That Wednesday, Melissa's article and pictures were featured on Page One of the community section. Mama bought ten newspapers and sent them to everyone she knew.

Melissa's idea had quick results, but Nicholas's idea was going to take a little longer to put into action. He had lots of details to work out, but he had all winter to do that.

4.

Blueberry Burgers?

When you're a blueberry guy, winter can be very long. And that winter was snowy on top of cold—really cold. Mama tried to warm things up with the blueberries they had picked all summer long: blueberry waffles, blueberry muffins, blueberry jam (on just about anything), blueberry syrup (on ice cream, especially), blueberries in corn flakes, oatmeal, cake, and pie, blueberries and cream.

Mama even put blueberries between the layers of Nico's

eighth birthday cake.

"You have to be kidding," Melissa said.

"I like it," said Hannah.

Nico said, "May I have another piece, please?"

"Aren't you getting tired of blueberry everything?" Melissa asked her brother. "I'm expecting Mama to serve us blueberry burgers any day now."

Nico shook his head. "They taste like summer," he told Melissa.

At holiday time, all four Prestons helped with gift-wrapping jars of blueberry jam, nestling them in sturdy boxes to send to cousins and friends who lived far away, or placing them in little baskets to deliver to near-by family, friends, and neighbors.

There was one basket for his teacher.

"I've heard about your family's blueberries, Nico," Ms. Allen told Nicholas when he brought in her basket with two jars of jam. "I can't wait to taste this."

"You'll like it," Nicholas said, sure that she would.

Nico smiled. The first step of his Big Plan had gone off without a hitch. But he would have to wait till spring for the second step.

5.
The Plan

When spring was just beginning to warm things up and make the days longer, Nicholas figured it was time to let his family in on his plan.

"Picking the blueberries last summer took us almost four whole weekends," he began one night at dinner. "We ended up with more blueberries than we could eat—or even give away," Nicholas reminded his family.

"Was it four whole weekends?" Mama asked.

"Four," Nico repeated.

"And that was with help from our neighbors," Daddy added.

"Uh huh," Nico agreed.

"What are you thinking, Nicholas?" Melissa asked.

"What if I got my whole class to help? I know the teacher will think it's a good idea. Ms. Allen loved the blueberry jam we gave her."

"Hmmm." Melissa smiled.

But Mama wasn't smiling. She looked worried. "That's a lot of kids to be looking after," she said. "One of them could get hurt." Then she added: "I'm not sure . . . "

"We could invite the parents to stick around," said Melissa. "They can help with the harvest if they want to, or they can sit on the deck and watch."

"That certainly would get the job done faster," said Daddy.

"And maybe we wouldn't have to eat blueberries every single day for the whole rest of year," said Melissa.

"I saved two jars of our jam for this," Nico told them with a smile that was part sneaky and part wise. "I'll bring them in for show-and-tell . . . and taste. Then I'll invite all the second-graders to help us this summer."

"We should set a date. So kids and their parents can plan for it," Daddy suggested. He looked at his phone-calendar. "How about Saturday, July 29?"

"Sounds good." Nico paused. "There's more."

"More?"

Nico nodded. "Once all the berries are picked, I'm going to ask everyone to leave some of their harvest with me. Then I'm going to sell the berries and donate the money to the community center."

Nico's parents were smiling.

"You know that big sign they have in front?"

"The one that shows how much more money they need to finish the playground, right?" Melissa asked.

"That one. All they need is $250.00 to finish buying the tiles for the playground's cushioned floor. I bet I can sell enough berries to earn $250.00."

"I bet you can," Daddy said.

On Monday, when it was sharing time in his class, Nico held up his jars and told his classmates: "This is blueberry jam from our backyard bushes. Everyone says we have the sweetest, tastiest, best blueberries in the world."

"Who says that," Brandon Big-Mouth asked. "Your parents?"

Nico didn't expect heckling. He wasn't ready with an answer.

"Really, Nicholas? The best blueberries in the world," Brandon teased.

Ms. Allen stepped in. "Why not taste the jam, Brandon, before you give Nico a hard time."

Nico nodded to his teacher and then went on to put a dab of Preston Jam on each of twenty-five crackers. He spread the crackers on a paper plate. Ms. Allen brought the plate around the classroom, and each kid took one.

"Ready, set, taste," said Nico.

The kids popped the crackers into their mouths, and smiles broke out.

"Nico's blueberries are the best," said Hannah.

"I guess they're okay," Brandon said.

"Thanks, Brandon."

That's how Nicholas convinced his entire class to come to his house to pick berries that summer. Even Brandon Big-Mouth!

6.

Bumper Crop

"It's going to be a bumper crop this year, even bigger than last year," Mama told Nicholas when the blueberry blossoms began to fall from the bushes and the first blueberries appeared.

"Bumper crop?" Nicholas asked.

"I don't know exactly what it means either," Mama said. "But it looks like we're going to have more blueberries this year than ever before."

"How come?"

"Many of our bushes are fully mature now, with berry production at the max."

"Good thing we've got some helpers lined up," Nico said.

"You bet!" said Mama, and she kissed the top of Nico's head.

A week or two later, Nico and Melissa were setting the table on the deck for a family "dinner al fresco," as Dad called it, when Nico heard a snapping sound coming from the woods.

"Listen," he whispered to Melissa.

She heard it too: the sound of branches twisting and twigs breaking underfoot. Could it be that Nico's bear is real? Melissa asked herself. She grabbed Nicholas and shoved him behind her as she reached for her camera. Nicholas peeked around his sister.

He saw the whole of the bear first: a big black shape

moving out of the woods and into their blueberry patch. Then he saw the paws, walking step-by-step through the patch. Bigger than he remembered. The claws alone—long and strong—could surely rip through anything.

"She's never, never ever, come all the way into the blueberry patch before. She always stays in the woods. Maybe this is a different bear," Nico whispered.

Nico saw the bear's snout, sniffing the air, smelling the veggies on their grill.

The bear saw Nico too, he was sure of that. She stopped and stood absolutely still. Silent. Staring. Was she his bear? What was she thinking? What was she going to do?

Up close like this she was scary. Nico never felt that before. But the more he watched her, the more he noticed the gentle way she held her head when she looked at him. And her soft fur. And her slow, quiet steps. He was pretty sure this was his bear.

"What should we do?" Melissa asked. Then she added,

talking to herself, "Look at this. I'm asking an eight-year-old what to do about a bear that's close enough to touch. Almost."

Just then, Mama came out. "Why are you two just standing, there?" she asked.

Nico pointed. Mama jumped into action. She picked up a handful of her metal gardening tools from an old box near the back door and started clashing them together.

She yelled too. "THESE ARE OUR BLUEBERRIES! YOU GO HOME!"

Melissa joined in, grabbing a metal pail and banging some of the gardening tools against it. She shouted too. "THESE ARE OUR BERRIES! OURS!"

Nicholas watched. The bear turned and headed right back into the woods, walking quickly, but not running. She turned around once, then disappeared in the trees.

"That bear is hungry," Mama said.

"She'd never eat our blueberries, Mama," Nicholas said.

"She would, Nico. And she will. And she could hurt us

if we get in her way. We'll have to do something about this."

"Something?" Nicholas asked.

"What?" Melissa asked.

"I'm not sure. I'll call the sheriff's office. There have to be some precautions we can take."

The next day, Mama and Daddy gave Nicholas and Melissa a talking to along with whistles on bright red ribbons to wear around their necks.

"Never! Never go into the yard alone. Never go on the deck or into the blueberry patch unless you've got your whistle on. If you see a bear or hear one, blow that whistle as loud as you can. Bears are afraid of loud noises. She'll retreat."

Mama pointed to some extra whistles on ribbons that were hanging next to the door. "In case any of your friends come by. And over there in the corner you'll find a bunch of old metal pots and pans. They'll make a lot of noise. Grab them and bang them with the metal spoons I've left nearby. That ought to keep the bear in the woods."

Nicholas was relieved. He was afraid the sheriff would tell them that the bear had to be shot.

A whistle. Some pots and pans. A couple of old spoons. Great idea.

7.

We Had A Deal.

Near the end of July, Nico headed down the deck stairs into the blueberry patch. In just a couple of days all his classmates would be coming to pick the first crop of the season.

Mama called, "Whistle!" Then she yelled for Melissa to come out and keep an eye on her brother.

Nicholas took his whistle and started walking among the bushes.

As he approached the last row, he saw that something was wrong. It was a corner bush. The branches were broken and hanging. The top was bent all the way to one side. And . . . and . . . all the berries were gone. Every berry.

Nicholas blinked his eyes hard. Once. Twice. Still the berries were gone. It couldn't be. He looked around. The other bushes were fine, but he took little comfort in that. He began to cry. No soft whimpering and sniffling. This was I-fell-off-my-bike crying. This was the-doctor-is-going-to-give-you-a-shot sobbing. This was your-best friend-is-going-to-the-town-carnival-and-you're-not wailing.

Mama ran from the deck. Nico couldn't catch his breath enough to talk. He pointed to the bush and started crying again.

Mama looked at the broken branches, the torn screening they'd put up over the bushes, the mess around the bush.

"I was afraid of this. A couple of neighbors said they thought they saw a bear sniffing around . . . "

Nico interrupted. "The bear?"

"Looks that way."

"No. No. It can't be. She'd never eat my berries. She just wouldn't. It has to be a different bear."

Mama held Nico. He wasn't crying anymore. He was angry. He was confused.

"I trusted her," Nicholas repeated. "We have a deal. I leave her berries, and I talk to her. Sometimes I read to her. She leaves our blueberries alone."

"We have a deal," Nicholas repeated sadly.

What could Mama say to all that? After a long while, she said, "The question is what are we going to do?"

"Maybe we can call animal rescue," Melissa half-asked, half-said.

Nicholas was horrified. He knew this time the bear had behaved badly. This time the animal people might have to take more drastic measures. "What will they do?" Nicholas asked. "They wouldn't hurt her, would they?"

"No, Nicholas. Sometimes they relocate animals. But it's more likely that they'll give us some ideas about how we keep the berries, the people, and the bear safe. Let's give it a try," Mama suggested.

The next day, Pam came from the animal rescue office. She told them that several bears had been seen in the area.

"See!" Nico said. "There are other bears."

"Let's listen, Nicholas," said Mama. She put her arm on Nico's shoulder.

The rescue worker continued. She said most of the

bears had been seen in the early evening. Most at trash cans. And, yes, they do like blueberries.

"What can we do?" Mama asked.

"Hanging some flags around the bushes would help keep them away. And some tin cans. Put them next to each other so they clang together in the breeze," Pam suggested.

Mama and Melissa ransacked Daddy's dresser and took all his old T-shirts. Mama stapled them onto plant stakes. They set up the T-shirt flags at the corners of the patch and hung tin-can mobiles along the outside rows.

Nicholas made a couple of signs that said:

NO BEARS, PLEASE.

Was that going to keep the bears out of the blueberries? Nicholas had another idea. The next day, wearing their whistles, he and Hannah, with Mama sitting nearby, settled themselves down in the middle row of the blueberry bushes, facing the woods.

He began: "BLUEBERRIES FOR SAL," Nico announced loudly.

Hannah held up the picture book so that a bear looking out of the woods could see it.

Nico continued, as Mama had so many times: "Robert McCloskey made the words and the pictures."

He started to tell the story. He didn't have to read it. He knew it by heart. As he recited, Hannah turned the pages, holding them open, facing the woods. "One day, Little Sal went with her mother to Blueberry Hill to pick blueberries."

He told how Sal's mother filled her large tin pail with blueberries while Little Sal ate most of the berries she picked.

Nicholas raised his voice as he reached the next page.

"This is the part you like best," Nicholas said loudly to the bear.

He continued reading: "On the other side of Blueberry Hill, Little Bear came with his mother to eat blueberries."

Nicholas pointed to the mother bear and her little cub in the pictures. "See?"

He finished the story. Hannah closed the book and announced to the woods: "You need to find Blueberry Hill and eat those berries. These are for people."

"Thanks, Hannah."

"Glad to help. Do you think this did the trick?"

"I do."

Then Nicholas waved to the woods and stood up. He hoped he had saved the blueberries and his big plans.

8.

That (Other) Plan

On July 29, the date they had set all those months ago, at 11 o'clock, the time they had set all those months ago, Nico was ready.

Lemonade and icy-cold water—check.

Paper cups and napkins—check.

Band-Aids, alcohol wipes, sun screen, bug spray—check, check, check, check.

Mama looked inside a small carton she'd put on the

table on the deck. She nodded to herself and closed the lid.

Nico waited in front of the house—ready to greet the first arrivals. No one was coming down the street, no one was coming up the street, and no one was coming around the corner.

He waited some more. Still no one. He shouted into the house. "What time is it?"

"Twenty five minutes after eleven," Melissa yelled back.

"They'll be here soon," Mama added.

But they weren't there soon. Nico kept his vigil; he waited for the phone to ring; he walked to the corner and back, went into the house, and came out again. At 12:30, there was still no one.

Quietly Nicholas climbed the stairs to his room. He closed the door and flopped down on his bed. Where were all his friends? They promised. They were part of the plan to help harvest the blueberries and help the town finish the community center playground. Every single one of them could not have forgotten.

They must have decided not to come. Probably Brandon Big-Mouth talked them out of it. Picking blueberries was hard work! Come to think of it, why would any kid give up a summer play day to help Nico out? This was his thing, not theirs. Why did he ever believe they would?

This was the worst day of his life. Everything had fallen apart. And it was too late for him to fix it. He had failed, and he'd be disappointing his family and letting the community center committee down, too. It got worse and worse the more he thought about it. What were the Prestons going to do with all those blueberries—just watch them rot away on the bushes? How was the floor of the playground ever going to get completed? Nico peeked out the window. Nope. No one. He buried his head back into his pillow.

There was only one thing he could do: never leave his room again. Just hide out here, sad, ashamed, embarrassed.

"Nico. Hannah's here," his mother called from

downstairs.

Mama sent Hannah up before Nico could answer. She opened the door.

"What's wrong?"

"What's wrong?" he repeated. "I'm a failure. There will be no blueberry harvest. The playground won't open this fall. All because of me."

Hannah didn't understand.

"Can't you see?" Nico said. "Nobody came to pick the berries. That's what's wrong."

"It's still early. We're supposed to be here at 1:00," Hannah said.

"No, Hannah. We were supposed to start at 11:00, but no one came."

"Nico." Hannah said calmly, "Ms. Allen sent out emails this week to remind us about the blueberry picking. It said to be at your house at 1 o'clock.

His mother called upstairs: "Nico, there are a bunch of

kids at the door. You better come down."

"Huh?"

It was the most amazing thing. Every one of Nico's second-grade classmates (except for a couple who were on vacation) along with at least one of their parents and maybe a sister or brother or two showed up, carrying bags and buckets and bowls and baskets. Even Brandon.

Melissa led them to the back deck. Mama welcomed

them. Nicholas left his room, climbed down the stairs, walked onto the deck and said, "It's great to see you."

Ms. Allen joined them. "Hello children," she said, patting Nicholas on the head.

He looked up at her. How could she be nice now? She had nearly ruined everything!

"I see you all got my email."

"Email?" Nico's father asked. "You sent out an email?"

Ms. Allen handed him the note. "It says 1 o'clock," Nico's father said. "We thought this was set to begin at 11."

"Oh dear," Ms. Allen said. "I must have typed it wrong. I meant to write 11:00. I was just stopping by now to see how you were all doing."

She looked at Nico. "You must have thought all your friends forgot."

What could Nicholas say? Melissa stepped in. "We're all here now. Let's get started."

To begin, Nicholas told everyone about the bear.

"We were back here doing homework. But something felt different. I thought I smelled something funny. Not really funny. Sort of stinky. And there she was. The bear. Giant size."

The kids all laughed.

"What did you do?"

"We made a lot of noise. Yelling and clanging. The bear turned around and went home."

"We showed her," Hannah said.

Nicholas nodded.

Mama handed out whistles from that box she had on the table. "That's why I'm giving each of you a whistle. Wear it, please. And if you see a bear . . . "

"Or smell one," one of the kids said.

"Or smell one," Mama repeated, "blow your whistle hard. Then leave everything right where you are and walk quickly into the house."

"Like a fire drill?"

"I guess."

The kids put on their whistles and practiced. Just in case.

It was a lot of noise.

It made a great photograph for Melissa.

Most of the moms and dads settled in on the deck and watched as the kids went to work. Melissa took some more photographs.

The kids worked hard, laughed a lot, sang songs, drank two gallons of lemonade, and took a break every now and then for a whistle-blowing rehearsal.

By four o'clock, the berries that were ripe on about half of the bushes had been picked. The kids got ready to leave, carrying bags and boxes and bowls and baskets that now were filled . . . and heavy!

It was time for Nico to tell his friends the rest of his plan.

He blew his whistle. Everyone stopped and looked around.

"Don't worry. Whistles aren't only for the bear. I just wanted to get everyone's attention."

Now all of the kids and all of the parents were looking at Nicholas. He took a breath, swallowed hard, then said, "You've got lots of blueberries—more than you thought you'd have, right? Probably more than you need. If you would leave one container behind with me, I'll sell those berries and donate the money to the new community center."

No one said anything, so Nico went on. "They only need $250 to finish the last bit of the playground floor. You know—that soft stuff they put on the ground so that if you fall, you don't get hurt."

The kids were nodding. The parents were smiling. Ms. Allen was beaming.

At the end of the day, Nico had two large cardboard boxes of blueberries filled to the brim.

9.

Blueberries For Sale

"That was some day, Nico," Mama said at breakfast.

"Uh-huh," Nicholas agreed.

"Everyone had fun. Everyone has blueberries. And you've got plenty to sell to raise money for the playground."

"But we've still got a lot of berries that will be ripening all through the season," Daddy added. "We're happy to give them to you to sell, Nico, but how are we going to get them picked?"

It was time for some new signs.

The next weekend, with help from so many neighbors, many more of the Preston's blueberries got picked. And Nicholas's blueberry supply was overflowing. He and Mama went to the Riley's farm and bought a slew of green pint-sized square paper baskets. They filled them up with blueberries, covered them with plastic wrap, and secured the wrap with rubber bands.

Nico was ready to open for business.

Nico set up a table and chair at the corner of their street. No one came by all morning. Finally, after lunch, a few neighbors walked past.

"Don't you want to buy blueberries," Nico called to them. "The money is for the community center," he added.

"I'd love to buy your berries, Nicholas," said Mrs. Fisher. "But we've still got plenty left from the day we picked them at your house. Good luck."

Oh! Nico got the message. This wasn't going to work. He packed up his sign and his stand.

10.
Sold Out

"I need a better location," Nico told his family at dinner. "Everyone around here already has our blueberries."

"Like where?" Melissa asked.

"How about the school yard?"

"That won't work," Mama said. "It's empty these days. The summer programs ended a week ago."

Nicholas tried again. "Maybe the park?"

"I don't think you're allowed to sell stuff in the park,"

said Daddy. "Sorry."

Nicholas looked disappointed. He tried again. "How about in front of the market?"

"They sell their own blueberries, Nico," Melissa said.

"Oh, yeah. Right."

Nicholas was out of ideas, but he went to bed still thinking. By breakfast time, he had a plan.

"I'm going to ask Mr. Collins. He has to say yes."

As far as anyone in the family could remember, Mr. Collins hadn't said yes to anything, ever! He didn't even answer his doorbell on Halloween. And if he did, he handed out pennies. Pennies!

Daddy offered to go with Nicholas.

"Nah. He's just down the street."

"I'll go with you, Nico," Melissa said.

Nicholas shrugged. Melissa grabbed a box of blueberries from the fridge and ran after her brother.

They knocked once. And waited. They knocked

again. At last Mr. Collins answered the door. He was tall, and Nicholas was feeling very small. But Mr. Collins pointed to the chairs on his porch, and the three of them sat down.

Okay, not so bad, Nico was thinking.

"What's up?" Mr. Collins asked.

"I need a place to sell our blueberries. I thought I could set up a table in front of your store in the mall."

"I don't think so. The mall doesn't allow sales outside the stores." Mr. Collins started to get up.

Nicholas wasn't ready for this. No. No. Mr. Collins couldn't just leave like that.

He had to listen to Nico's plan and see what a good idea this was. But how was Nicholas going to persuade him? What could he say that would change Mr. Collins's mind?

Melissa handed Nico the box of berries and pointed toward Mr. Collins with her chin.

Finally, Nicholas spoke. "Oh. That's too bad. They really are the best blueberries ever." Nicholas held out the box of berries.

Absentmindedly, Mr. Collins took a few berries and popped them in his mouth.

"They are good."

"Uh-huh," Nico agreed.

"But I'm pretty sure there are rules about selling in the mall's public space."

"It's for the community center," Nicholas said.

"What do you mean?"

"All the money is for the community center. So they can finish the floor of the playground."

"Charity? It's for charity?" Mr. Collins scooped up a big handful of berries.

As he chewed, Nico thought he saw him smile.

The next day, Mama drove Nicholas, a brand new sign, a folding table and chair, and twenty-four little boxes of blueberries to the mall. Nico set up in front of the canoes on display outside of Collins Sports.

BIG **FAT** fresh & juicy BLUEBERRIES! Buy a box and build our new community center $3

Mama stuck around but stayed in the background. Nicholas insisted on doing it himself. By lunchtime, the mall was crowded. Nicholas sold out by two o'clock.

"Good job, Nicholas. That's a lot of money for the community center."

"Seventy-two dollars."

"Yes," said Mama, then added, "how about we get some lunch?" Nicholas clutched his earnings.

Mama laughed. "Don't worry, this is my treat. I know

the money is to donate."

The next day, Nicholas did a lot of arithmetic. He counted the empty green boxes he had. He eyed the carton-loads of blueberries. With a little help from Melissa, he figured out how many packages he needed to sell to raise $178.00.

He was ready for his next trip to the mall.

All Nicholas had to do was sell the forty-five boxes he had brought with him, and he'd make $180.00. That, plus what he had from last weekend would be just what was needed to complete the playground floor.

In three hours, he did!

That week, the headline of the Our Community section of the local paper read...

11.
Labor Day

The all-new, all-improved Raccoon River Community Center Playground (with its soft and safe floor!) was set to open on Labor Day. The traditional town parade would end at the Center at noon, and a full afternoon of "fun for everyone" was planned.

Sue Michaels, President of the community center, called the Prestons on Sunday to ask if Nicholas could be at the community cnter an hour earlier "for photographs and interviews and such." Nico couldn't. He had promised to ride with his friends in the red-white-and-blue bikes brigade—an important part of the parade. "Maybe you can get there a few minutes early?"

"I'll try," Nico said.

Turns out he was late. One of the clowns on stilts tripped over a beach ball that had drifted into the parade route, and everything had to stop for five full minutes.

"Now I'm going to be late," Nico told Hannah. "What's taking so long?"

"I guess that's how long it takes to pick yourself up when you're wearing stilts," Hannah said.

There was a pretty big crowd surrounding the playground when Nico and his friends finally arrived. Everyone was there. Waiting. He saw Mama and Daddy, Melissa, snapping pictures like crazy, Ms. Allen, the school principal, lots of neighbors.

This really was a big deal!

Nico straddled his bike and wondered what they were waiting for. The mayor was standing beside a sparkling golden ribbon at the entrance to the playground. He walked toward Nico and his pals. He put out his hand. "Nicholas Preston?"

Huh? Nico didn't get it. Why was the mayor asking for him? Nico nodded. "I'm Nico."

"Please follow me, son." The mayor leaned over to Hannah and asked her to look after Nicholas's bike. Did he wink? Nico thought he saw the mayor wink.

As they were walking, the mayor gave Nicholas a pair of scissors. "You'll be cutting the ribbon and officially opening the playground. How's that?"

Nico didn't answer, so the mayor kept talking. "Before that, there's a brief presentation. Is that okay with you?"

Nico nodded.

A guy in a suit and tie was standing near the center of the ribbon when Nico and the mayor got there. The man took a whistle out of his pocked and blew it hard. Everyone stopped talking.

"Ladies and Gentlemen," he began.

He looked around.

"Boys and Girls," he added.

"I'm Philip Ross, President of The Chamber of Commerce. We will begin the celebration of our new community center by officially naming Nicholas Preston, third grader at Raccoon River Elementary School, *The*

Top Businessman of the Year. He has grown a small family hobby into a genuine business, and he's used that business to contribute to our town's community center. We are proud of him. We admire him. We congratulate his parents and his sister. And we thank them."

He handed Nicholas a plaque, shook his hand, and stepped aside.

Now it was the mayor's turn.

Nico was pretty uncomfortable, but he looked at Mama and Daddy who were smiling and cheering. Nico could see how proud they were. And Hannah—she was just about jumping out of her shoes with excitement.

"My fellow citizens," the mayor said. "This is a beautiful moment for our town. One of our own, a young boy, an eight year old, has done something unselfish and wonderful to benefit our town now and for generations to come. We should all say thank you!"

He turned to Nicholas. "Will you cut the ribbon and

open up our new playground, Nico?"

Nico held the over-sized scissors tight and cut the ribbon. The two sides of the ribbon fluttered in the gentle wind and glittered in the sunshine.

Everyone cheered.

Nico took a small bow.

"Where should we hang your plaque, Nico?" Mama asked when they got home.

Nico didn't want to talk about that now. He had something to do. He took the plaque from his mother and headed outside—into the blueberry patch. He put on a whistle and walked past the last row of nearly-empty bushes toward the woods. Nico held up the plaque, so that the fancy writing faced into the woods.

"I got this today," Nico announced. "It's because I sold some of our blueberries and gave the money to the community center so they could finish the playground floor."

Nicholas took a deep breath. Did he smell the bear? He stared into the woods, looking hard between the trees. Did he see the bear? He listened carefully for sounds of her walking on the leaf-covered floor of the forest. Did he hear her?

Maybe. He kept on talking.

"I wanted to show this to you. It's a kind of award. You helped, you know. You didn't eat all the berries when you could have. I know you must have been extra hungry. Next year, I'll leave lots more berries for you. Maybe other stuff, too. Deal?"

Nico waited and watched. He thought he saw the bear in a clump of trees farther back in the woods. Yes, he was certain. She was thinking about next year too, Nico knew, even as she was getting ready for the winter.

12.

Scripting A New Story

Nicholas and Hannah made it a point to bike past the playground whenever they could. The soft black tiles that covered the ground looked fine under the layer of leaves and pine cones and acorns.

Nico and Hannah didn't see any scratches. They knew that when the first snow fell, and then the next, and the next, the tiles would hold up nicely. None of them would crack or lift up. And when spring came around, the floor would be all set to do its job—protect kids from scraped elbows and bloody knees and black-and-blue behinds.

It felt good to bike through his town and know he had helped to make this happen. It was a feeling he wanted to last. More than that, he wanted to do more.

"What you did was really nice," Hannah said.

"I didn't do it alone you know."

Hannah smiled. "I have been thinking . . ." Hannah began.

"You, too?" Nicholas said.

"Uh-huh."

They were just riding past the old abandoned Plaza Theatre with its windows painted black, its ticket booth tattered and leaning, and its marquee spelling out some message with so many missing letters you could not figure out what it said.

"What do you think it says?" Hannah asked Nico,

pointing up at the marquee.

Nico read: "FAY UN"

Hannah tried: "F. A. space space space Y. space space U. N."

"That's what I said, Hannah. FAY UN."

"Let's figure it out," Hannah said. "UN. That could be sun, bun, run, fun. What else?"

"I think it's FUN."

"Okay. Now the other word: F. A. blank blank blank Y. What's that?"

They stared at the letters. It suddenly came to Hannah. "It's FAMILY. F. A. M. I. L. Y."

"Family fun," Hannah said. "Maybe there was a show here for the whole family. A movie. A concert. Something."

"Family fun," Nico repeated.

"I think that's something Raccoon River could use a whole lot more of," Hannah said.

Both Hannah and Nico nodded . . . and smiled.

END.